Finding Eden

A Journey of Remembrance:

Three Sacred Stories, One Shared Return

Derny-Jean

A Dedication of Thanks

To Rahma B. — the light at the fork,

Where choices divide and courage walks.

To Dayane J. — the voice that spoke

When silence trembled beneath its cloak.

To Lilie — the Treasure, quiet and true,

A gem of grace the world once knew.

To Sherlie — the Legacy that still breathes,

Rooted in time like ancient trees.

To Afna K. — the poet's flame,

Whose words remember from whence we came.

To Mila D. — a light dimmed, fuel still burned,

Energy reclaimed, and purpose returned.

And to all ears that listened deep,

All voices that stirred me from sleep.

To Wolf — my pack, my kindred howl,

In darkened woods, your presence is soul.

To Kwame D. — the moment truth stood still,

And clarity rose against my will.

To Marc-Elie E. – the sudden sight,

A mirror turned toward inner light.

To those who teach without a name,

Whose quiet truths still burn like flame.

To the mute — who gestured truth

When I had no words, just restless youth.

To the blind — who showed the way

When all my vision led astray.

To Port-de-Paix — where echoes rest,

A ***Paix*** that hums within my chest.

And to this garden, vast and wide,

The Earth, our Eden, where dreams abide.

To all of you, I bow, I see—

Your light, your gift, your legacy.

Thank you.

Foreword

By the Voice of the Storyteller

There are stories passed down from generation to generation, carved into stone, recited in sanctuaries, and whispered by firesides. But then there are stories that rise—not from tradition, but from memory. Not from doctrine, but from longing.

Finding Eden is such a story.

It doesn't claim authority over ancient texts, nor does it seek to replace the faith that brought you here. It asks a question so old it feels like a breath you forgot you were holding: **What if the Garden was never lost—only enlarged, and forgotten?**

This book does not arrive with certainty. It arrives with soil under its nails, dust on its sandals, and a deep reverence for both the wound and the wonder of being human.

It dares to hold hands with scripture and question. With Eve and Adam. With history and the hush beneath it. It listens for the voice before the division, and the wisdom that still hums through the roots of the Earth.

Whether you read this through the lens of faith, curiosity, or quiet ache—know this: Eden may not be behind you. It may be waiting for you to see it again.

So walk slowly. Listen carefully. And return—not to doctrine, but to presence. Not to fear, but to breath.

Because here, we remember what was never truly lost.

—The Storyteller

A Note to the Seeker—Whatever Path You Walk

You may come to this book carrying beliefs, questions, or long-held stories. You may come from Christianity, Islam, Judaism, African spirituality, the earth-centered traditions of your ancestors, or none of these at all. You may come certain. You may come wounded. You may come searching for what the world has not yet named.

Whoever you are— **_You are welcome here._**

This is not a book of answers. It is a remembering. A return. It does not ask you to abandon your path. Only to pause... and listen for the voice beneath the voices. The breath beneath the scriptures. The truth before the division.

This story is for those who suspect there's more. For those who feel the imbalance, the fracture, the ache to come back into wholeness.

It honors the beauty that exists in many traditions— but it also dares to ask: what if the most sacred parts were forgotten, buried under conquest, fear, and silence?

You do not need to agree with everything here. But if something in you stirs, softens, or opens— follow that thread.

Because Finding Eden isn't about replacing your faith. It's about deepening your roots. And remembering that before the names, before the divisions, before the blood— we were all just breath.

Act I

What Was?
What Is?
What Could Be?

Prologue – The Echo Before the Voice

Long before there were cities, before ships crossed oceans and
men etched their names into stone, there was a song.

Not loud, not boastful. Just a song—soft, steady, full of knowing.

It moved through the hands that planted, the eyes that watched,
the arms that held.

It shaped the rhythm of life in ways no monument ever could.

And though it was never written in history books, it never
stopped playing.

But the world listened to drums instead.

So the song waited—not in silence, but in patience.

It waited for the ones who would stop running long enough to
hear again.

Who would ask different questions.

Who would wonder what we might become...not if we kept going,
but if we finally returned.

This is the story of that return.

Of a man and a woman.

Of a fire and a garden.

Of the voice we forgot...

and the journey we can still begin.

The Inheritance

They told me I was born stained—

not by mud

nor by mistake,

but by a story written long before I breathed.

A fall, they said.

A bite, a break,

a curse passed down like blood through the veins of every child.

Not for what I did,

but for what someone else did.

And somehow, I was to own it.

Carry it.

Be humbled by it.

Be ashamed because of it.

They taught me to memorize the fall

but not the mercy.

To tremble at justice

but not to dance in grace.

To inherit the guilt

but not the embrace.

I asked them—

what of the love God showed?

What of the mercy that clothed the naked,

even after the fig leaves wilted in shame?

What of the grace that walked in the cool of the day,

still calling the lost by name?

No, they said.

That cannot be passed down.

Only the stain, not the healing.

Only the curse, not the kiss.

As if wrath was stronger than the hands that shaped the stars.

But I wonder—

did we inherit the curse,

or did we inherit the belief in the curse?

Did we fall, or were we taught we had fallen

so we would forget how to rise?

What if God's mercy was always larger than the fall?

What if the first breath was still holy?

What if we were never meant to carry

another man's shadow,

but only our own light?

They set the world stage with tragedy as the opening act,

and called it truth.

But I say—

let the curtain rise again.

Let us remember the mercy

buried beneath the rubble of inherited shame.

Let us reclaim the grace

they told us we could not keep.

Because I was not born to wear another man's sin.

I was born to remember

the love that was mine

before the story was stolen.

The World We Built Without Her

On a sunlit morning in the Dominican Republic,

the vibrant streets pulsed with life—

fruit vendors calling,

engines sputtering,

children laughing in bursts.

It was eleven a.m., and the day seemed ordinary—

until it wasn't.

Three of us stood frozen.

Not by heat, not by awe—

but by the cold, unyielding gaze of a gun.

Time didn't slow.

It stopped.

But in that pause, there was no hatred in my heart.

Only a sorrow so deep,

it felt ancient.

As if I had witnessed this before—

not here,

but in a field stained by the hands of a brother.

The same act Cain could not undo.

The same cry Abel's blood still echoes.

It wasn't just a robbery.

It was a reenactment—

of forgetting.

Of what happens when we lose the face of the other

and replace it with fear.

These young men weren't much older than boys.

And something—

something bigger than any of us—

had driven them to this moment.

As a Marine, trained in reaction,

every muscle could've sprung to action.

But something older than training rose within me.

A knowing.

Not loud.

Not heroic.

Just still.

I handed them what they demanded—

not with fear, but with compassion.

Not because I was weak—

but because I saw what the world had done to them.

To all of us.

That night, sleep didn't come.

Only questions.

And images I couldn't unsee:

– A boy with a weapon he shouldn't know how to hold.

– A world that forgot how to hold him.

I laid still beneath the fan blades,

listening not to their hum—

but to the ache beneath it all.

I began to see not threats, not sides—

but stories.

Wounds that were never ours, passed down like heirlooms.

Grief coded into tradition.

Fear normalized as protection.

And I wondered:

How much of this sorrow did we mistake for strength?

How many times did we call trauma "legacy"?

That day cracked something open in me.

The shell of certainty.

The armor of assumption.

And beneath it all—

I found the softest voice.

A whisper I had ignored for years.

Not hers exactly—

but close.

It asked nothing of me,

except to look again.

Not just at the world—

but at what we built

when we left her behind.

The Mirror of Belief

The concept of **Pacifism** didn't arrive with thunder.

It came quietly—

in boot camp of all places.

Not in a sermon,

but in a passing conversation—

the kind that slips between commands and exhaustion.

At the time, I didn't call myself a **Pacifist**.

I was ready to fight.

Ready to kill, if I had to.

That's what I had signed up for.

That's what I had been trained to do.

But somewhere between the shouting and the drills,

a question lodged itself like a seed.

Not from weakness—

but from awareness.

I started facing questions I'd never dared to ask:

About the God I was taught to serve.

About what was truly sacred.

About whether obedience was the same as truth—

and whether following orders

meant turning away from wisdom.

I held onto Christianity then—tightly.

But the grip was loosening.

And just as it began to slip,

Islam appeared.

Not as a replacement.

Not as rebellion.

But as a mirror.

It gave me another language to wrestle with God.

Another image of surrender.

Another path to weigh.

And then I found myself sitting with all three—

Christianity, Islam, and Judaism.

Not as houses I lived in,

but as structures I was trying to see from the outside.

And what I saw disturbed me.

Each began with breath—

but moved quickly to blood.

From gardens to graves.

From divine presence to divine punishment.

Sacrifice.

Wrath.

Obedience tested by suffering.

It echoed too closely the world I saw around me—

a world where pain proved devotion,

where violence could be holy

if it had the right name behind it.

I stood back and looked again.

And what struck me

was not just what was there—

but what was missing.

Africa.

The first cradle.

The breath before any book.

In all the sacred texts I was handed,

Africa was either background or forgotten.

As if humanity's story didn't begin where it truly began.

As if we leapt forward from distortion
and called it creation.

And I wondered:
If the stories begin after the forgetting,
what are we truly calling holy?
Are we preserving a revelation—
or protecting a fracture?

Maybe the fire from the sky,
the wrath that split cities,
the tests of loyalty through blood—
maybe those were not the voice of God,
but the echo of our own wounded hearts.

Maybe by the time we wrote these stories,
we had already lost something.

Something feminine.
Something whole.

The deeper I looked, the clearer it became:
I wasn't caught between religions.
I was caught inside an inherited imbalance.

A way of seeing that silenced the other half of the voice.

And my soul began to whisper:

There must be another way.

One that begins not with sacrifice,

but with breath.

Not with fear,

but with wisdom.

Not with domination,

but with care.

That whisper has never left me.

And I've come to believe—

it was her voice all along.

The Voice We Forgot

You've come back quiet.
That's how I know you're ready.

I never asked you to stay.
Only to bring me with you.

But you left with fire—
and I held the flame.

You carved your face in stone,
etched your victories into history,
built your towers, your temples, your thrones.

But you left no space for my name.

I read your stories.
They were loud.
They were proud.
They were yours.

They spoke of conquest and creation,
of chosen ones and holy wars.

But I remember the part you didn't write.

The goodbye you never said.

The cradle you never turned back to see.

You built cities,

but not home.

You spoke of heaven,

but forgot the womb that bore you.

So now—

if you're willing—

tell me the part you buried.

Not the tale of what you built.

Tell me what it cost.

Tell me of the sons you sent to war

without teaching them how to weep.

Tell me of the women who waited,

whole generations,

watching the stars for a sign you remembered.

Tell me of the silence

that followed your songs.

Tell me why you feared softness

as if it were weakness,

when it was the only thing that ever made you whole.

And tell me—

now that you are tired,

now that the drums are fading—

can you still hear it?

That first voice.

The one that sang through soil and seed.

The one you knew

before you learned to conquer.

I have waited—

not in silence,

but in memory.

Now, I ask you not to defend—

but to remember.

What We Carried and What We Left Behind

He sat with her words like stones in his hands.

Small.

Heavy.

Undeniably real.

He didn't rush to speak.

For once, he knew better.

He let her voice echo inside him,

not as a wound—

but as a mirror.

"I came to believe," he said,

"that a man must go.

Must prove himself.

Conquer.

Bring something back."

He paused, staring down at his palms

like they were maps he had followed blindly.

"But no one said,
'Take her with you.'
No one told me your voice
was part of the map."

He paused, eyes lowered.
"Maybe they didn't say it...
because they thought I already knew.
Because I was first—
and they trusted my silence
was something sacred.

They followed my footsteps,
not realizing I was still lost."
He looked down, hands open,
like he was still trying to catch something
he had dropped a long time ago.

"I left to find meaning," he said.
"To become something.
To make my mark.
But I didn't know I already had it—
in the laughter of the children
in the stillness of your knowing,

in the breath before the battle."

He looked at her—

not to explain.

But to confess.

"I didn't forget you.

I didn't know you were missing.

And that may be worse."

He closed his eyes,

and in the silence,

he felt all the moments

he had called strength

when they were really fear.

All the times he had spoken

when he should have listened.

The wind moved between them—

not to fill the space,

but to bless it.

Nothing more needed to be said.

But he said it anyway.

"I'm tired of returning to ruins.

Tired of rebuilding what never needed to fall.

If there's still time—

I want to build with you."

She Who Remembers the Stars

She looked past him—
through time,
through memory,
through the thousand steps he'd taken
without her shadow beside him.

And when she spoke,
there was no softness lost—
only the veil of silence lifted.

"You went alone."

She said it gently.
But the truth landed like stone.

"You left with fire,
but not with balance.
With maps,
but no memory.
With questions,
but not the courage to ask me."

She turned her face to the sky,

but her words fell to the ground—

like seeds that had waited centuries to be planted.

"You walked into new worlds

with your hands clenched—

not to greet,

but to take.

Not to listen,

but to name.

You saw wonder,

but called it yours.

You saw difference,

and treated it as lesser."

She looked at him now—

not to wound him,

but to wake him.

"This is what happens

when one half of the voice

carries the whole story.

You call it civilization.

But I see the harm beneath its shine.

You call it history.

But I see all that was silenced."

She knelt, touching the soil.

Her fingers pressed into it

like a mother feeling for a heartbeat in her child.

"We were meant to go together.

Had you taken me—

my patience,

my listening,

my memory—

those new lands might have become teachers,

not trophies.

Those new faces,

not foes."

She stood again—

not towering,

but rooted.

"And now you speak of the stars.

Of leaving Earth behind.

Of beginning again.

But if you go

with only half the truth—

if you carry only conquest into the cosmos—

you will not arrive.

You will invade.

And the stars...

they will dim."

Then her voice softened—

not with sorrow,

but with resolve.

"I am not here to stop you.

I am here to walk with you.

Not behind.

Beside."

She offered her hand.

"And this time—

if we go as one,

with open hands

and open hearts—

we may not just survive the journey.

We may be received."

The First Step Together

He didn't rise right away.

Her words still echoed—
not just in the room,
but in the hollow places inside him
he had spent years avoiding.

For the first time,
he felt no urgency to respond.
No need to repair,
to explain,
to be right.

He just breathed.
And in that breath—
he found her rhythm.
Quiet.
Steady.
True.
Then, softly:

"I didn't know what I was missing.
But now I can feel the silence
I used to walk with."

He looked at her—
not for permission,
but in reverence.

"I've led too many marches
that ended in ruins.
Too many steps taken
without listening.
Too many victories
built on forgetting."

His voice trembled,
not with fear—
but with truth.

"But if there's still time...
I don't want to walk ahead anymore.
I want to walk with you.
Not for peace in name only.
But for something real.

Something whole."

He reached out—
not with force,
but with faith.
He offered his hand
as one offers a seed to the soil—
hoping it still remembers how to grow.

She nodded—once.
Slow.
Steady.
The way the earth agrees
without needing applause.

And she placed her hand in his.

They said nothing more.
There was no need.
Because now,
for the first time in the story of their kind,
they began together.

One step.

One rhythm.

One future—

woven from both voices.

The Turning Within

The path ahead was open.
But they didn't walk it yet.

Because before the journey could continue,
they had to become still enough
to hear what had never been spoken aloud.

They sat together beneath the dusk.
Not in silence—
but in listening.

To the parts of themselves
they had both ignored.
The shadows inherited.
The myths mistaken for truth.

He turned inward—
and saw not just the battles,
but the boy who had learned
to measure his worth by winning.
The one praised for not crying.

The one trained to protect,

but never taught how to be held.

She turned inward too—

and met the weariness

of always being patient,

of being expected to understand,

to bend,

to carry the memory no one asked for.

There was no blame between them.

Only recognition.

"I thought I had to be strong all the time," he said.

"And I thought I had to stay soft,

even when it broke me," she answered.

Their words didn't echo.

They landed gently—

like rain returning to soil.

And then, they wept.

Not out of shame—

but release.

The kind that doesn't collapse,

but clears.

The kind that makes room

for something new.

They sat like that

through the night.

Not planning.

Not building.

Just remembering

who they were

before the forgetting.

Not warriors.

Not saints.

Just human.

Still.

And ready.

Welcome to Eden

The night wrapped around them like a warm shawl,

the stars blinking slowly—

watching,

not judging.

Their breath slowed.

Time didn't stop.

But it softened.

And in that stillness,

they touched something older than language—

a silence that remembered everything.

Then, without sound or sign,

the ground beneath them began to glow.

Not bright—

just a gentle shimmer,

as if memory itself

had risen from the soil.

They looked down—

and saw it.

Light blooming from the roots of the earth.

Not fire.

Not conquest.

But memory—alive and patient.

Shapes began to form.

Not with sharp edges,

but like dreams made visible.

A tree—

older than scripture.

Older than grief.

Its branches cradled constellations.

Its roots reached deep into forgotten songs.

In its trunk,

images flickered.

Not of war.

Not of thrones.

But of children dancing in circles.

Of elders singing in dusk-light.

Of hands building not monuments—

but homes.

Of a people who knew

that wisdom doesn't roar—

it hums.

It wasn't a vision of what was.

It was a remembering

of what could have been.

And maybe—

still could be.

He reached toward the tree.

But the light passed through his fingers—

not to be grasped,

only received.

She placed her hand on the ground beside it.

And the tree pulsed gently,

as if to say:

"I remember you. Both of you."

Then, just as quietly,

the vision faded.

The light sank back into the earth—

not gone,

just waiting.

They sat there,

still beneath the stars.

And they knew.

Magic was never something to seek.

It was something you unlocked—

by remembering wholeness.

Not a return to the beginning.

But a return to what was true

before we turned away.

The Return Is Yours

This story was never meant to end with the final chapter.

Finding Eden is not a tale of the past—

it's a call to remember what still lives beneath our feet,

within our breath,

and between each other.

The questions that follow are not tests.

They are invitations.

To pause.

To unlearn.

To feel.

To imagine.

To return.

Let them unsettle you.

Let them open doors you forgot were there.

Let them whisper what the world has tried to silence.

Because Eden is not behind us.

It is within reach—

when we walk with both voices.

Reflection Questions

What have I mistaken for strength that was actually a survival wound?

What parts of me have been praised for their silence, their toughness, their endurance—when what I truly needed was to be heard, held, and healed?

Reflection Questions

Whose voice have I inherited—and whose have I forgotten? In my beliefs, my history, my ambitions... whose stories do I carry forward? And who did I leave behind? What truths might be waiting in the silence?

Reflection Questions

What would it mean to live without the myth of domination? If I stopped measuring progress by control, conquest, or competition—what new kind of civilization could I begin building today?

Reflection Questions

Am I walking with both sides of the voice?

In my relationships, decisions, and dreams... am I making space for both wisdom and action, memory and movement, the feminine and the masculine? Or is one half carrying what was meant to be shared?

Reflection Questions

If Earth was never mine to own, only to know—how would I walk differently?

How would I move, build, plant, and speak if I truly believed the ground itself was listening? Would the stars welcome the footsteps I take now?

Reflection Questions

What if the sacred didn't begin in scripture—but in breath? Before religion, before rules, before sacrifice—what if the Divine first appeared in the stillness of presence, the beauty of care, the balance of life? Can I find Eden there again?

Reflection Questions

What cycles of harm have I called tradition?

What beliefs or practices have I passed down or accepted simply because they were inherited—not because they were true, whole, or life-giving?

Reflection Questions

What would I create if I no longer feared softness?
If tenderness was my compass, and imagination my tool, what kind of world would I begin building today? What Eden waits on the other side of my return?

A Whisper at the End

If you've come this far,

then you've already begun your return.

Finding Eden was never just a story I wanted to tell—

it was a memory I wanted to awaken.

Not of a perfect place,

but of a sacred way of being

we once knew... and can know again.

In these pages, I laid bare my journey—

through belief and doubt,

through war and stillness,

through forgetting and remembering.

I did not write this as one who has arrived,

but as one who is walking beside you.

Still listening.

Still learning.

Still reaching for balance in a world tilted by forgetting.

If something stirred in you—follow it.

If something challenged you—sit with it.

If something softened you—trust it.

Because this world doesn't need more monuments.

It needs more hands held.

More stories told with both voices.

More builders who remember the roots.

May you carry this story forward—

not as mine,

but as ours.

With breath,

with courage,

and with care.

Act II
Settling Into Balance:

A Pilgrimage Home

Prologue

The sun was low, golden, stretching shadows across the red soil. And there, beneath the old baobab tree— one whose roots had tasted the first rains—they met. Not by plan, not by force, but by something older than memory.

He came from the mountains, she from the rivers. Each had walked their own path, learned in silence, in struggle, in longing. He carried questions that had once turned to stone. She carried stories no one had asked to hear.

They had been living a story shaped by storms and survival, by love and loss. It wasn't blame that sat between them, but the ache of what had been carried alone. And now, the quiet knowing that together, it could be different.

They sat without a word. For a while, the wind did all the speaking. Rustling the leaves above, brushing the dust between them. Then, slowly, their eyes met. No accusation. No blame. Just knowing.

He looked at her hands—rough, strong, sacred. She looked at his face—tired, gentle, open.

"I thought I had to carry it alone," he said softly. "I thought I wasn't allowed to carry it at all," she replied.

Then silence again. But this time, not empty.

Together, they placed their hands on the earth. And she breathed out first, then he. As if releasing centuries. As if forgiving the story they didn't write—but could now finish.

And the earth listened.

Two

Their hands still touched the earth. Warm. Alive.

He broke the silence first, eyes scanning the horizon where distant mountains met sky.

"We built a lot," he said. "Stone on stone. Walls, roads, towers. We chased the stars. We made the world move faster."

She nodded slowly, her fingers brushing the soil. "And yet, something always leaned. Tilted. Like it was reaching but never resting."

He glanced at her, the weight of his voice thick with years.

"It wasn't that we didn't know what was good. We wanted it— peace, beauty, joy. But we reached for it without you. Or worse, we reached while holding you down."

She didn't answer at first. She didn't need to. The truth sat between them, patient and old.

Then she whispered, "I saw what you built. I never hated it. I only wished we built it together."

A breeze stirred the dust around them.

He looked down. "Maybe that's why even the high places feel empty. The top was never meant to be a place to stay. It was meant to be shared—or maybe even passed down."

She smiled softly, not with her lips, but with her whole presence.

"The view is better when you're not alone."

And just like that, without command or apology, they began to speak of what could be made new— not from stone, but from understanding. Not from power, but from balance. A home, not a tower. And this time, they'd build it together.

When We Forgot

There was a time when the circle broke.

When the branches, proud and reaching, turned from the root
that fed them.

We built altars to our own reflections— named them progress,
called them power.

We made mothers into servants. Turned wisdom into silence.

Carved borders into the skin of the Earth and called it order.

Children were taught to forget— not through cruelty, but through
noise.

And the tree stood still. It watched generations run from its
shade in search of light that burned too fast.

Eve wept—not in anger, but in the ache of being unseen. And
Adam, chasing shadows of greatness, forgot the warmth of her
presence.

Still, the earth remembered. Still, the wind whispered. Still, the
tree waited.

And so forgetting grew, until even the stars felt distant.

The Call

The roots beneath them ran deep— deeper than memory, deeper than the names carved into borders.

This tree had stood long before kingdoms, before flags, before the forgetting.

And now, Adam and Eve sat beneath its branches— not as figures of shame, but as the first voices rising again to speak with clarity.

They did not speak to each other alone. They spoke to the tree. To the earth. To the wind that carried their words to every forgotten corner.

High in the branches, an old owl stirred. She had watched empires rise and fall. But never had she seen a silence this full of truth.

"Let this be known," Adam said, "we were never enemies. We were never meant to be divided."

Eve placed her palm against the trunk, as if greeting an old friend. "We were not born into blame. We were born into beauty. And though pain came, it taught us. Though distance grew, we survived."

Adam turned to the sky, which now held the colors of fire and dusk.

"To our children across the world, those who built towers and those who tended seeds, those who remember and those who have forgotten— this is your story too."

Eve's voice softened, but reached farther than mountains.

"Africa is not the shadow of your past. She is the cradle of your breath. The Mother of your becoming. Do not look away. Come home—not to a land, but to a truth."

The tree groaned softly in the breeze, a sound like old bones stirring.

"We are the first," Adam said, "but we are not above you. We are with you."

"We are one," Eve echoed. "The roots do not envy the branches. The branches do not blame the roots. All belong. All carry life."

They looked at each other— no longer two voices, but one harmony.

And from that moment, the story no longer belonged to one book,

or one people,

or one version.

It belonged to the tree.

To the wind.

To the children.

To all.

The Further We Grow, The More We Forget

From the shade of the great tree, soft footsteps approached.

Not loud or hurried, but with the quiet certainty of those who

knew they were welcome.

The children came in ones and twos. Some barefoot,

some with books tucked under arms,

others with devices still glowing in their palms.

They came from cities,

from villages,

from places where languages shifted like the wind—

but here, they understood.

They sat in a ring around Adam and Eve.

Not because they were told to.

But because something in them remembered.

One child, her hair full of beads that sang when she moved,

raised her hand.

"Why did no one tell us this version of the story?"

Eve smiled,

not with pity but with warmth.

"Because many forgot.

And some feared what remembering would change."

Another boy, his skin like polished mahogany, frowned.

"Is this why we feel so broken sometimes?

Like something's missing,

but we don't know what?"

Adam nodded.

"You feel it because you carry both the pain of the past and the

pull of a better future.

You are the bridge."

A child from across the sea, his accent thick and different, leaned

forward.

"But if we're all from the same tree, why do we fight so much?

Why do we act like the branches don't belong to each other?"

Eve looked up into the limbs of the baobab.

"Because the farther the branches grow,

the easier it is to forget they come from the same root.

But forgetting is not forever.

Remembrance is a choice."

Then a quiet girl in the back,

no older than seven, whispered,

"Can we... tell the story differently now?"

Adam looked at Eve.

She looked at the children.

Then they spoke together:

"Yes. And not just tell it—live it.

One branch at a time."

And so the circle grew.

Not in size,

but in understanding.

The tree did not grow taller—

but its roots sank deeper,

fed by truth,

carried by voices once silenced now rising again.

The Original Design

As the children sat, the circle began to change.

One by one,

they pulled from their baskets,

their bags,

their memories—

fruits and foods grown in soil both near and far.

They laid them gently at the base of the baobab,

not as offerings,

but as invitations.

A girl from Ghana brought golden mangoes,

their skins still warm from the sun.

A boy from Japan unwrapped a parcel of rice cakes,

soft and sweet with red bean paste.

From the Caribbean came a young girl with jerk-spiced plantains

and stories of spice ships and stolen roots.

A tall boy from Sweden shared cloudberries,

rare and bright like little bursts of light.

Another child from Ethiopia offered injera,

its tangy scent rising like memory,

paired with stews rich with tradition.

The girl with the singing beads clapped her hands.
"Look at all this!
We're like a garden—
every flavor, every color, from every corner."

Adam's eyes softened.
"This was always the design.
The Earth gave each of you something different—
not to compete,
but to complete."

Eve picked up a piece of bread and broke it in two.
She handed one half to the child beside her.
"When you taste each other's food,
you taste each other's story.
And when you share it,
something inside you expands."

A boy from South Africa stood up,
holding a pot of chakalaka.
"We cook with what we have,"
he said.
"Spices, tomatoes, beans. It's fire and warmth.
I didn't think others would care about our food.

But now...

I want everyone to try it."

Then a quiet girl from northern China held out a dumpling.

"My grandmother used to say food remembers what we forget.

Every fold is a story."

One child from the Middle East,

holding dates and rosewater sweets, added softly,

"Maybe peace starts with a shared table."

And so the tree, once a silent witness to humanity's journey,

became a place of reunion.

Not just through words—

but through taste,

memory,

and the joy of learning from one another again.

The Tree of Remembrance

The circle grew quiet once more. The fire of the shared meal
softened into glowing embers.
Adam turned to the children.
"This tree was here before us.
It held our silence, then our return.
But we must not just remember.
We must plant what will outlive us."

Eve stepped forward with a small seed in her hand.
"It is from the fruit of our remembering.
It has tasted the stories,
the questions,
the flavors,
and the tears."

Each child brought something to mix into the soil:
A handful of spice.
A crumbled leaf.
A drop of oil.
A pebble.
A cloth.
A whispered hope.

Together,

they pressed the seed into the earth, t

heir hands overlapping in a circle of unity.

Adam spoke softly,

"Let this tree grow not to divide, but to remind."

Eve added,

"Let it bear the fruit of balance—

where no voice is above,

and no root is forgotten."

And something shifted.

Not in the sky.

Not in the ground.

But in them.

They were not just branches of a broken story.

They were gardeners of a new one.

And they knew—

whatever came next,

they would grow it together.

The Embrace of Our Beginning

Days passed.

Seasons would follow.

The seed they planted had not yet sprouted,

but the soil knew.

The earth remembered.

And so did they.

The children went back to their lands—

not to forget, but to carry the circle with them.

In their cooking.

In their questions.

In their courage to listen.

In the quiet moments when they would touch the ground and

whisper,

we are one.

And beneath the baobab,

Adam and Eve remained.

Not to rule.

Not to teach.

But to hold space—

for anyone who chose to return.

Because the story wasn't ending.

It was just now being told together.

And beneath their feet,

the roots carried a quiet joy—

a hum older than language,

a pulse that said,

"Welcome back."

And you who read this—

you who carry questions,

you who feel the tremble beneath your feet—

this story is now yours.

What will you plant?

Act III

Whispers From the Garden:

An Invitation to Remember What Was Never Lost

Introduction

This is not a rewriting of scripture.

This is a remembering.

Before we inherited the language of shame and sacrifice,

before we learned to fear the face of God,

there was a garden.

And in it, breath was given freely.

Love was not earned.

Life was not a transaction.

This is an invitation to return—not with guilt, but with wonder.

To listen for the ***original question*** that still echoes through the

silence:

<u>"Where are you?"</u>

Let these whispers guide you home.

The Question in the Garden

The fire cracked like old bones settling.

A child sat cross-legged at my feet, eyes wide,

the way only a soul still close to the truth can be.

"You said God never asked for blood," the child said.

"But don't all the stories say He did?"

I poked the embers and smiled—not because it was funny,

but because it was familiar.

"That's what men say," I answered.

"But if you listen carefully—

not to the noise,

but to the whisper behind the stories—

you'll notice something different."

The child leaned in.

"God asked Adam and Eve only one question:

'Where are you?'

Not 'What have you done?'

Not 'What will you offer to make it right?'

Just—

'Where are you?'"

I tossed a twig into the flames.
"That question wasn't for judgment.
It was for reunion.

There was no sword in God's hand,
only sorrow.
And even then,
not sorrow at them—
but sorrow at what they would now face,
without fully understanding who they still were."

The child looked down at their hands.
"So... the pain wasn't punishment?"
"No,"
I said gently.
"It was the world adjusting to their new way of seeing.
They left innocence—
not because they were wicked,
but because they began to see God as separate.
That's when the fear began.
That's when shame taught them to hide."

Reflection Questions

When did I first begin to believe that love must be earned?

Reflection Questions

What have I mistaken as punishment that might actually be preparation?

Reflection Questions

Do I still hear the question **"Where are you?"** echoing in my life?

The First Offering

The child was quiet for a while, tracing their finger in the dust.

The fire cracked between us.

"If love was never something to earn..."

the child began,

"...why did Cain offer the fruit of the field?

Why did Abel bring the lamb?"

I stirred the ashes slowly.

"They were trying to return,

to find their way back to a voice they no longer heard as clearly.

When a soul cannot feel the closeness of God,

it begins to think it must do something to be seen again."

The flames danced lower now.

"Cain wasn't evil,"

I said.

"He was hurt.

He wanted to be accepted.

But instead of listening to the silence,

he listened to the thunder in his own chest."

"So God didn't want Abel's lamb more than Cain's harvest?"

"No,"

I said.

"God wasn't asking for either.

That was the misunderstanding."

The child whispered,

"Is that why the ground cried out?"

"Yes.

Because Abel's blood remembered what Cain forgot:

that we are not here to take from one another.

We are here to keep one another.

To guard what is sacred.

And nothing is more sacred than **life**."

Reflection Questions

What have I sacrificed that was never asked of me?

Reflection Questions

Have I mistaken competition for closeness with God?

Do I believe protecting life is the most sacred act of worship?

The Dream Beneath the Ashes

That night,

the child dreamed.

They stood in a vast, empty field.

In the center,

an altar made of rough stone.

Two offerings lay upon it:

a basket of golden grain,

a silent lamb.

Then, a voice—

not loud,

but clear—

spoke without words:

"Who taught you to believe I needed this?"

Two figures appeared:

Cain and Abel.

They placed their offerings but never met each other's eyes.

The child stood between them,

placing a hand on each.

The altar cracked.

Beneath the stone—

soil.

And in the soil,

a seed.

"This is the true offering:

To bury what divides you,

and tend to what might grow between you."

When the child awoke,

a green sprout had broken through the ashes near the firepit.

Revelation Question

What if the true altar God waits for is not built of stone, but of reconciliation—planted between the places we've let division grow?

By the River, We Remembered

The river ran quiet,

though not still.

It carried with it the echoes of Eden,

soft and patient,

as if waiting for them to return—

not with fear,

but with truth.

Adam sat on a smooth stone near the bank,

his hands thick with earth.

Eve stood barefoot in the water,

her fingers tracing ripples that never resisted her touch.

They had not spoken to God in some time—

not because God had left,

but because they had wrapped themselves in the silence of

shame.

Then,

like wind threading through leaves,

the voice came—

not from above,

but within and all around.

God:

"Why have you hidden your hearts from Me?"

Eve turned,

startled not by the sound,

but by its gentleness.

Adam bowed his head,

tears mixing with the dust on his hands.

Adam:

"Because we thought You were angry."

God:

"Were you not the ones who walked away?"

Eve:

"We thought we had to earn our place again...

We thought... we had to give something.

A sacrifice.

A sign."

The river shimmered.

A breeze kissed her cheek.

God:

"You were given breath before you ever spoke a word.

You were loved before you ever understood love.

Did I ever ask you for blood?

Or did I ask you to walk with Me in the cool of the day?"

Adam's chest heaved.

Adam:

"Then why the pain? Why the toil? Why the thorns?"

God:

"Not punishment—

preparation.

You chose to taste what you weren't ready to carry.

So I gave you instructions,

not to curse you...

But to keep you from being devoured by your own hunger."

Eve: (whispers)

"And childbirth?"

God:

"A doorway.

Not a curse, but a passage through which creation continues.

Your body became a garden—

and even gardens ache before they bloom.”

She wept,

but it was the weeping of remembrance—

not grief.

Eve:

“Then we misunderstood You.”

God:

“No.

You misunderstood yourselves.

And in your shame,

you began to imagine Me in your image—

a god to be appeased,

not a Parent to be known.”

The river lapped gently at Adam’s feet.

God:

“But I have not changed.

I am still walking.

Still calling.

Still loving you before you name Me.”

They said nothing more,

only listened.

And in that moment,

by the river,

they remembered:

They had never been cast out of love—

only invited to see more of it.

Eden was never behind them.

It had been enlarged—

unfolding across the whole Earth.

The rivers,

the forests,

the deserts,

the skies—

all part of the same sacred garden.

We didn't lose Eden.

We forgot the Earth was Eden,

and we were its stewards.

But when we remember—

when we walk with care,

speak with reverence,

and tend what was entrusted to us—

the garden stirs.

And the magic returns.

What if Eden was never lost—only renamed, resold, and ravaged—and the garden we've been searching for is the very Earth beneath our feet?

If the whole Earth is Eden, how would I live, build, and care differently—knowing every step I take is on sacred ground?

The Tree That Remembers

The morning was quiet.
The child touched the sprout near the fire—
it leaned into their hand.

The Old Storyteller stood beside them,
sipping from a wooden cup.

"Will it grow?" the child asked.

"That depends,"
the elder replied,
"on whether we remember."

They walked through the mist
until they reached the edge of the village.
There,
stood a tree—
ancient, scarred, still.
"Some say this is where Cain wept.
Some say it grew from Abel's tears.
Maybe both.
Maybe neither.

What matters is:

it still grows.

Because life,

even after betrayal,

still answers the sun."

The elder placed seeds in the child's hands.

"Not every offering must be burned.

Some must be planted."

And so they walked.

Back into the world.

With new soil beneath their feet.

"Where Are You?"

You were not born beneath a curse,

but beneath a sky that knew your name

before you spoke.

You were not carved from guilt,

nor stitched from shame,

but breathed into—

by a Love so deep,

even silence could not contain it.

You were not made to kneel in fear,

but to walk—

barefoot,

beloved—

through the garden of communion,

with no altar but your heartbeat,

no offering but your being.

But somewhere,

between what was given

and what was feared,

a new story took root—

one that taught you to earn

what was already yours.

They called it sin.

They called it fall.

But really,

it was forgetting.

And still, the question echoes

through soil and sorrow,

through scripture and sleep:

"Where are you?"

Not to accuse,

but to awaken.

Not to condemn,

but to call you home.

So pause.

Lay down the burden of borrowed beliefs.

Let the sword of shame rust in the grass.

Breathe.

And remember:

You were always meant

to live,

to love,

to grow—

not as a debtor,

but as a child of the garden,

answering a voice that has never stopped

calling you by your real name.

Where are you?

Now,

answer with your life.

Final Invitation

If you have heard the whispers, plant something sacred. Begin again.

Author's Note

To all fellow seekers, and to humanity as one,

I invite you on a journey to rediscover the roots of truth, where life began in Africa, and where our first stories were written. If we seek the truth, let us look back to the cradle of humanity. Today, as violence persists and the value of the soul seems diminished, we must ask: **Do we truly hold God's message?**

Let us come together, like rivers flowing into an ocean, seeking the true orientation of humanity. This journey transcends boundaries, leading us to a wisdom that can heal and uplift us all.

I warmly invite you to join me, hand in hand, heart in heart, as we uncover and embrace these timeless truths. Together, let us shape a future rooted in understanding and unity, for our sake and for generations yet to come.

Afterword: A Historical Reflection

A Radical Remembering

Finding Eden is not a revision of sacred tradition. It is a restoration—a soul-etched journey to what may have been buried, misnamed, or silenced.

1. Reframing the Eden Narrative

Where tradition often frames Eden as a paradise lost due to disobedience, Finding Eden imagines it as a consciousness forgotten—a garden not guarded by swords, but by forgetfulness. Here, exile is not punishment, but a shift in how we see ourselves and the Divine.

2. Reclaiming the Forgotten Feminine

Eve is no longer the temptress, but the rememberer. The story reframes her not as the one who led us astray, but as the one whose silence marked the world's imbalance. This echoes both ancient matriarchal memory and modern theological revisioning that call for sacred equality.

3. Recentering Africa

While many sacred texts begin after empire and conquest, Finding Eden remembers what came before: Africa, the cradle of breath and balance. It is a spiritual act of decolonizing the narrative and honoring the soil from which humanity rose.

4. Questioning Sacrifice

The book wrestles with the inherited theology of blood and redemption. It wonders whether God ever asked for blood—or if we projected our brokenness onto the Divine. In doing so, it returns us to a time where communion meant walking, not appeasing. Where the sacred began with breath, not sacrifice.

5. Living Story as Sacred Memory

Rather than fixed law, Finding Eden treats the story as seed—alive, evolving, echoing. This return to oral tradition, parable, and poetry places the sacred back into the hands and hearts of everyday people, and invites each reader to become a co-rememberer.

In Closing

Historically, Finding Eden stands as both critique and invitation. It does not reject faith. It breathes new life into it. It does not deny the sacred—it reclaims what has been overshadowed by conquest, by empire, and by fear.

It is not the final word. But perhaps, it is the first breath of remembering.

May we walk lightly. May we speak truth with tenderness. And may we see Eden—not in some distant past or promised future, but in the soil beneath our feet.

—The Storyteller